I'm Reading About OKLAHOMA

The Sooner State!

GALLOPADE

by Carole Marsh

Printed and Manufactured in Peachtree City, GA., USA
www.gallopade.com

Book design: John Hanson

Editorial manager: Janice Baker

Oklahoma is a great state.

It is one of a kind.

What makes Oklahoma special?

Let's read about it

and see!

NATIVE AMERICANS

Who lived in Oklahoma first?

Native Americans did!

They moved around to find food.
They hunted in Oklahoma's woods.
They fished in Oklahoma's rivers.
They gathered fruits and seeds and nuts.

EXPLORERS

The first explorers came to Oklahoma in 1541.
They came from the country of Spain.

Francisco Vásquez de Coronado was their leader.
He and his men were looking for cities of gold!

SETTLEMENT

In 1889, many settlers moved to Oklahoma at once.
They called it the "Land Rush."
They made new towns.
One of them was Oklahoma City!

In the "Land Rush," settlers
raced to the land they wanted.
They claimed it as their own!

Oklahoma City
Oklahoma City
OKLAHOMA CITY
INDIAN TERRITORY.
1890.

STATEHOOD

Oklahoma was the 46th state to join the United States of America!

Isn't it great,
to be a state!
I bet Oklahoma
could hardly wait!

Oklahoma became a state in 1907.

Oklahoma
The 46th State
Here we are!

FLAG

I am the state flag.
I was adopted in 1925.

What colors am I?
Blue. Brown. White. Green.

Look at me.
What else do you see?

I fly high over the state of Oklahoma!

OKLAHOMA

CAPITAL

Say hello to Oklahoma City,
the capital city of Oklahoma!

There is an important building in Oklahoma City.
It is the State Capitol.
Oklahoma's laws are made there!

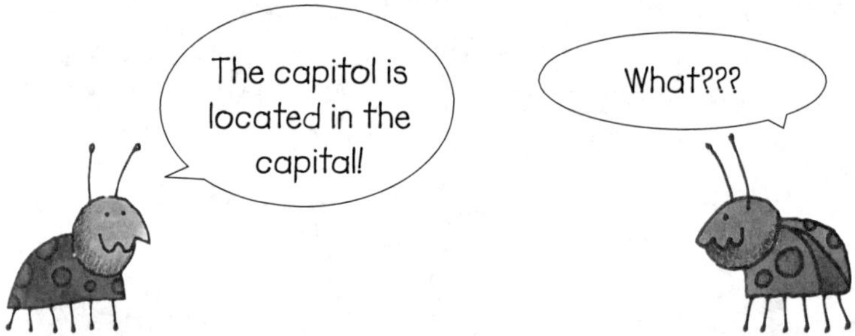

Capitol

SEAL

I am a seal,
but I am not the State Seal.
If I were, I would be very important.
I would be stamped on many official papers.
(Ouch, that might hurt!)

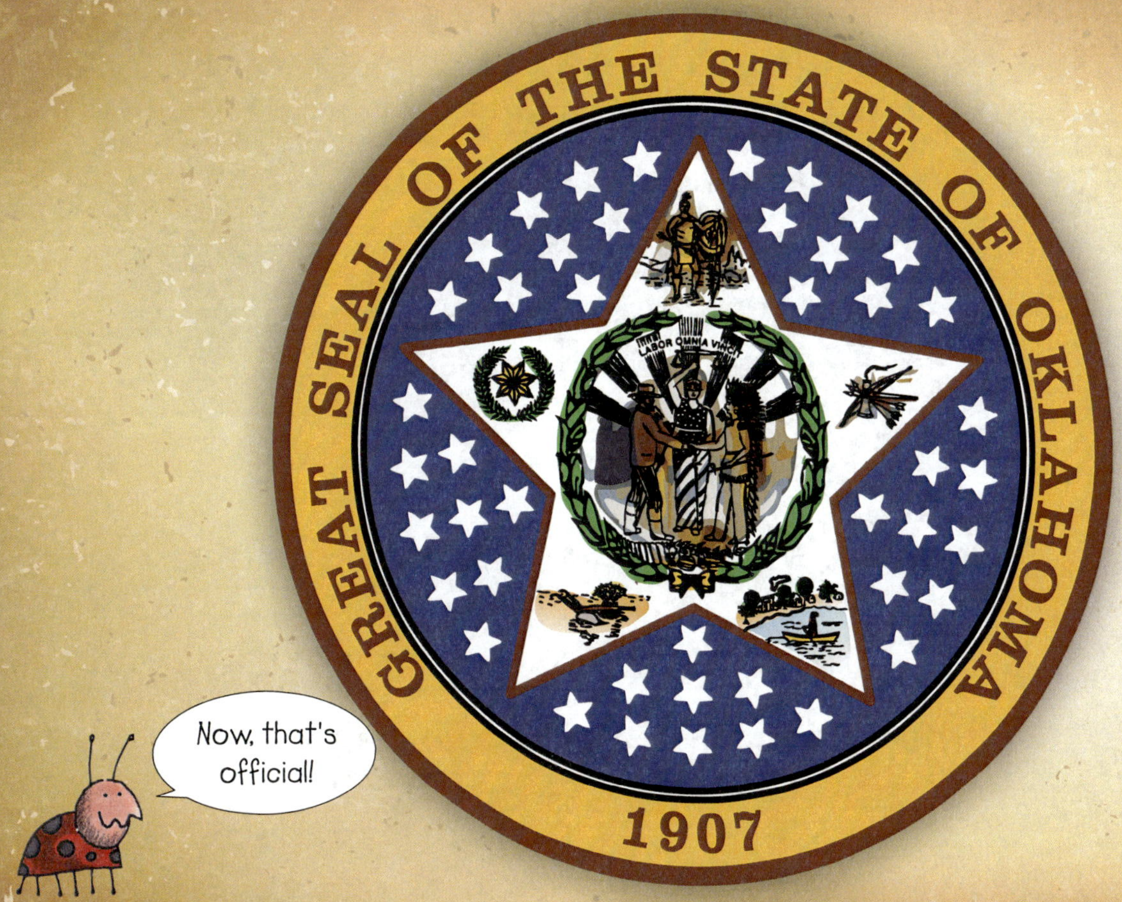
GREAT SEAL OF THE STATE OF OKLAHOMA
LABOR OMNIA VINCIT
1907
Now, that's official!

NICKNAME

State nicknames are fun!
State nicknames are great!
They share fun facts
about each state!

Oklahoma's nickname is "The Sooner State."

Some people could not wait to claim Oklahoma's land. They started the "Land Rush" early and got there "sooner"!

The Sooner State

BORDERS

Look at Oklahoma.
Oklahoma is in a region called "the Southwest."

Oklahoma borders six other states.
Find them on the map!

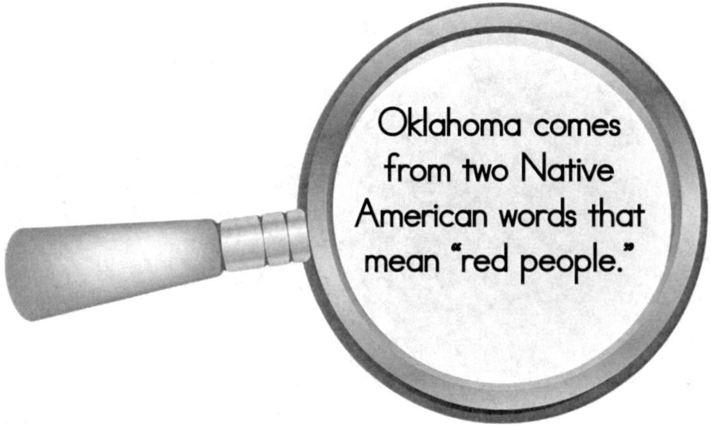

Borders

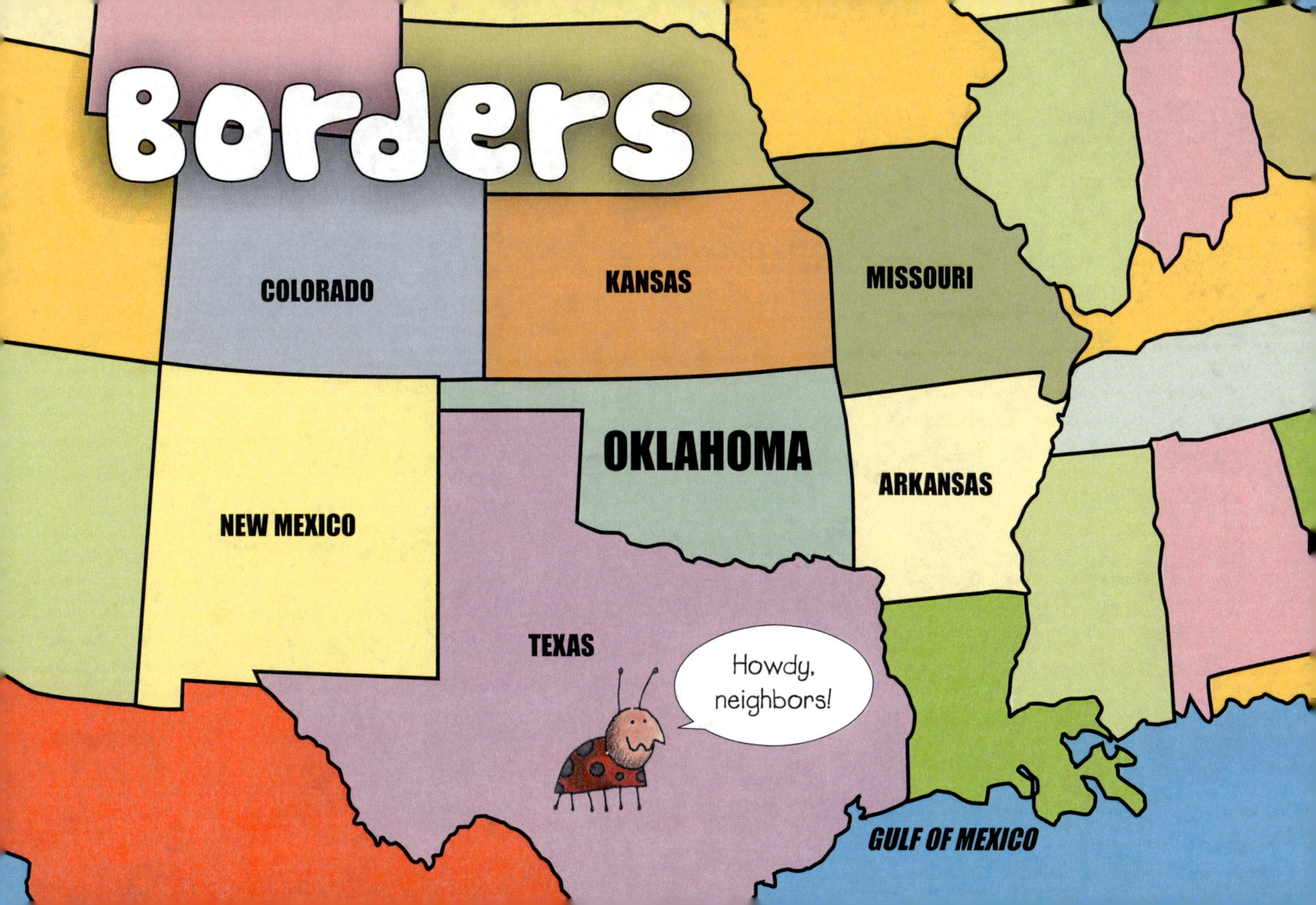
COLORADO
KANSAS
MISSOURI
OKLAHOMA
ARKANSAS
NEW MEXICO
TEXAS
Howdy, neighbors!
GULF OF MEXICO

COUNTIES

Oklahoma is divided into 77 counties
Counties are a form of local government.
Counties provide services that people need!

Those services include:

Schools Parks Libraries Police
Firefighters and More!

Counties

OKLAHOMA'S CAPITAL, OKLAHOMA CITY, IS IN OKLAHOMA COUNTY.

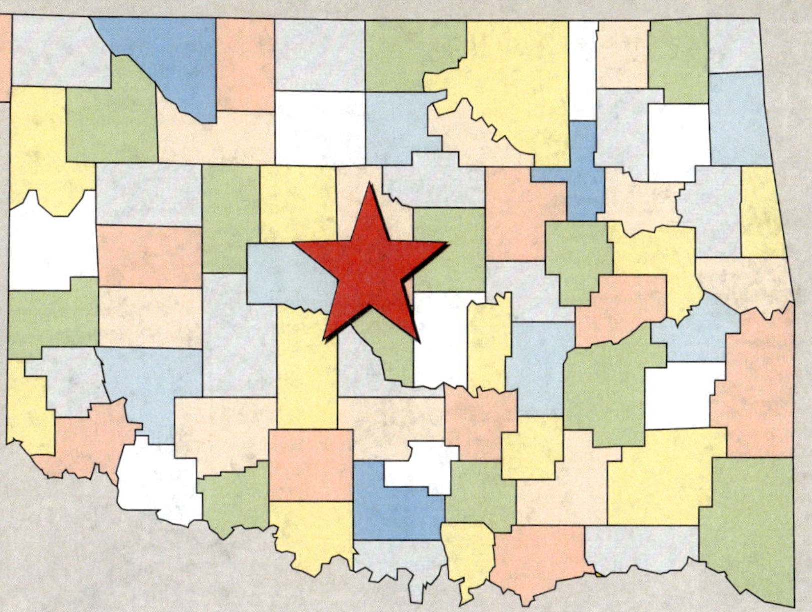

PEOPLE

Many famous people

Jim Thorpe

Olympic gold medalist and one of the greatest athletes of the 20th century

Wiley Post

First pilot to fly solo around the world

Sam Walton

Founder of Walmart and Sam's Club

call our state home!

PEOPLE

Maria Tallchief

America's first prima ballerina

Mickey Mantle

Regarded as one of the greatest players in baseball history

Wilma Mankiller

First female chief of the Cherokee Nation

Scissor-tailed Flycatcher

I am the state bird, and I fly
over Oklahoma, proud and high.

As I fly, up in the sky,
I flap my wings to tell you "Hi!"

The Oklahoma state bird
is the Scissor-tailed Flycatcher.

BIRD

Oklahoma Rose

FLOWER

I am the Oklahoma Rose.
I am the state flower.

I grow where it's warm and sunny.
I climb over shrubs and walls.
I help make Oklahoma beautiful!

Look at me! Smell me!
But don't touch my sharp thorns!

Redbud

TREE

I am a Redbud—I'm the state tree.
All over Oklahoma is where to find me.

My bark is brown.
I have heart-shaped leaves.
I bloom pink blossoms in early spring.

I stand up straight, big and tall.
Don't climb too high—it would hurt to fall!

Honeybee

I am the Honeybee.
I am the state insect.

I might sting you if you bother me,
But really, I am your friend.

I carry pollen from flower to flower.
I make honey.
I help Oklahoma crops grow.

BZZZZZZZZZZZZ!

INSECT

Tallgrass Prairie

PRAIRIES

Oklahoma is home to tallgrass prairies. The thick, golden grass sways in the breeze.

The prairie is flat. There are no trees. It stretches as far as the eye can see!

Oklahoma's prairie is home to many animals:

Deer **Bison** **Birds** **Armadillos** **Coyotes** **and More!**

Ouachita Mountains

MOUNTAINS

Oklahoma's Ouachita Mountains are the place to be.
Hiking, fishing, camping—
fun for you and me.

If you were to climb
to the top of a tree,
you'd have a beautiful view to see!

Ouachita National Forest

FORESTS

Oklahoma has many beautiful forests.
The Ouachita National Forest is the largest one.
It is in southeast Oklahoma.

This habitat is home to many animals:

Birds **Deer** **Turkey** **Fish** **Owls** **and More!**

The Ouachita National Forest is named after the Ouachita Indian tribe.

The Golden Driller

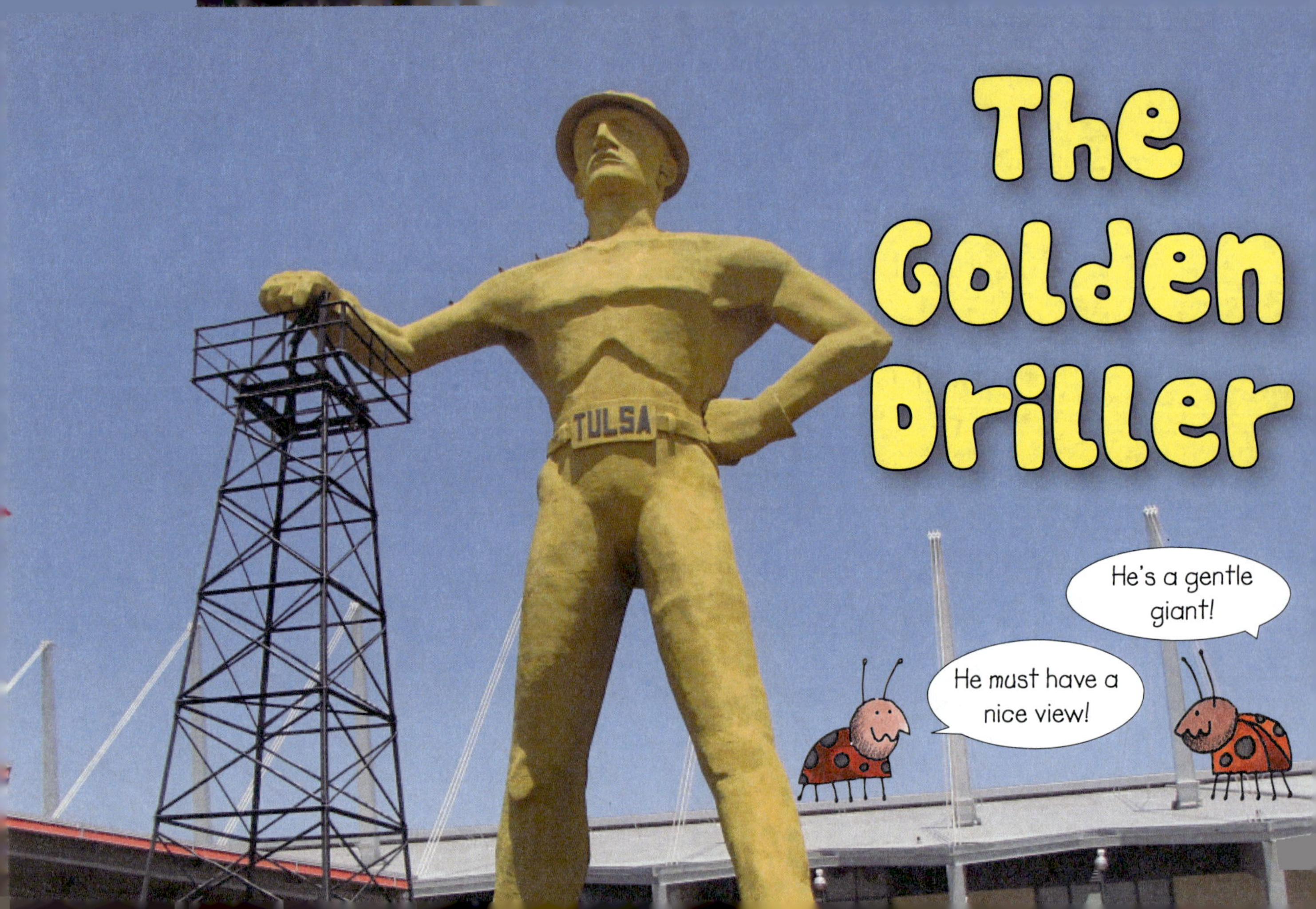

LANDMARK

The Golden Driller is a large statue.
It is a statue of an oil worker.
The statue is 76 feet high—that's very tall!
The Golden Driller is in Tulsa.

In 1979, Oklahoma made
The Golden Driller the state monument!

Oklahoma Crops

AGRICULTURE

Oklahoma has many farms.
Why?
Because Oklahoma has good soil and a warm climate!

Some of the top crops grown in Oklahoma are:

Wheat **Hay** **Soybeans**
Nursery Plants

Sports in Oklahoma

SPORTS

Baseball! Basketball! Football!
Oklahoma has it all.

Whether you like to watch or play,
You are sure to have a ball!

Redhawks **Blazers** **Wranglers**

Sooners

Broncos

& More!

Oklahoma: Home of Indian Territory

CLAIM TO FAME

Oklahoma was part of the
original Indian Territory.
Five major tribes moved to Oklahoma.
Those tribes were:

Cherokee Chickasaw Choctaw
Muscogee Seminole

Native American culture
still influences Oklahoma
today!

GLOSSARY

climate: weather conditions in an area over a long period of time

habitat: a place where plants or animals naturally live

influence: to affect something or someone else

laws: rules made by the government

pollen: a yellow powder that helps plants make new plants

regarded: to think of something or someone in a specific way

region: an area that has similar characteristics

settlers: the first people in an area

solo: something done by one person

territory: an area of land under the laws of a ruler